THE SIDE DEAL

ALL IN BOOK 1

LACEY CROSS

Contents

CHAPTER 1

I FAKE A LAUGH at Senator Miller's tired joke. It's the same one he told at last year's gala. When I take a sip of my champagne, it tastes like expensive disappointment, just like everything else at the Wellington Foundation Gala.

"Excuse me," I murmur, slipping away before he launches into his standard speech about tax incentives.

Three hundred people in designer evening wear fill the ballroom, their voices creating a hum of practiced enthusiasm. I weave between clusters of Seattle's elite, nodding at familiar faces without making eye contact long enough to invite conversation.

Catherine Wellington appears beside me, her diamond earrings catching the light from the massive chandelier overhead. Her fingers brush my bare shoulder. "Shannon, darling! You look absolutely radiant tonight."

I curve my lips upward—the same angle I've perfected through fifteen years as Mrs. Robert Matthews. "Thank you, Catherine. The event is lovely, as always."

Her gaze darts past me, scanning the crowd. "Where is Robert hiding? I simply must discuss the new wing funding with him."

Of course she must. Everyone wants to discuss something with my husband. Robert Matthews, partner at Blackstone & Associates, the man who can make million-dollar decisions over cocktails and somehow make it look effortless.

I gesture toward the far side of the room. "He's near the silent auction tables." At least I think he is. I haven't seen him in—I check the time on my phone—forty-seven minutes, not since he whispered something about municipal bonds before drifting away.

As Catherine leaves, I sip my drink and spot Robert across the room. Oops, guess he's not by the silent auction tables anymore. He's standing with three men in identical tuxedos, hands animated as he speaks. The chandelier light catches his silver hair. He's sexier and more fit at forty-eight than when we got married.

I set my glass on a passing server's tray and smooth my hands over my scarlet dress. The familiar weight of expectation settles across my shoulders as I prepare to endure another evening of meaningless small talk.

Carol Price's voice cuts through the chatter. "Shannon!" Her heels click-clack across the marble as she approaches, clutching her champagne flute like a microphone. "You're just the woman I was looking for. We need someone to chair the spring benefit planning committee."

I straighten my spine. "Of course. I'd be happy to help."

Carol explains venues and catering options, and I nod while my eyes glaze over. This morning, I stood in my walk-in closet, touching silk blouses and tailored slacks I wore when I used to work. My old marketing portfolio sits in a box on the top shelf, untouched for a decade. The last campaign I designed won an industry award, and now the trophy collects dust in our guest room.

"...so if you could have the preliminary budget ready by next week, that would be great."

"Absolutely." I have no idea what I just agreed to. I'll email her tomorrow and tell her I was tipsy and need the information again.

She squeezes my arm and disappears. I grab a champagne flute from a passing server, not because I want it but to occupy my hands.

Robert materializes by my side. "There you are. Having a good time?"

I adjust his crooked bow tie and lie. "Yes, I was just talking to Carol about another committee."

He nods and shifts his gaze toward the bar. "James wants to discuss something with me. I'll be a while."

"Of course, love. Take your time."

His lips brush my cheek, and then he's gone, cutting through the crowd, stopping twice to shake hands before reaching James.

I stand motionless as conversations swirl around me. The room feels too warm and too loud. In ten years, I'll be in this exact spot, in a different designer dress, having this same conversation.

My chest tightens. I need to get out of here. I walk toward the ladies' room.

The bathroom's soft lighting flatters even the harshest features. I stare at my reflection. My brown hair is styled in loose waves, and my makeup enhances my features without being obvious. The velvet dress cost more than most people's monthly rent.

I look exactly like what I am. A bored trophy wife.

I reapply my lipstick and return to the ballroom. Robert's holding court near the bar, gesturing with his whiskey glass. I don't think James is getting much time to talk to him.

The second champagne glass empties too quickly. I set it down and check my phone. At least another hour until I can leave without drawing attention.

When Robert finds me again, I've memorized the floor pattern.

"James wants to go for drinks to talk more." He checks his watch. "If you want to leave, he said he'll take me home."

My shoulders loosen. "Okay, love. I'm tired and will probably be asleep as soon as my head hits the pillow."

He kisses my cheek again, this time even more briefly, and walks towards James without glancing back.

Eight years ago, we would have raced home from these events and torn our clothes off of each other before we were barely in the door. Now we coordinate separate rides and pretend not to notice the time when the other slips into bed.

I retrieve my wrap and clutch from the coat check and step outside. The valet brings my car around, and I slide into the driver's seat.

Seattle transforms into a constellation of lit windows against dark buildings. The car's GPS says forty-two minutes to home, but a restlessness claws at me. I can't face our sterile house yet. I'll just lie awake staring at the ceiling for hours.

As I drive, Robert's words from three nights ago pop into my head. "If you ever wanted to explore being with someone else, I'd be into that. As long as you tell me every detail." He whispered it against my neck in the dark, and I laughed it off at the time. Now, driving through the sleeping city, his suggestion makes me wonder. Where would I even meet a guy? I wouldn't fuck anyone we know. But the fact that I'm even thinking about this makes me realize I need a change.

My discontent builds until I'm yanking the wheel toward the next freeway exit. I don't know what I plan to do. I drive through parts of Greater Seattle I never visit, where the buildings are older and the neon signs promise things my neighborhood doesn't offer.

When I'm stopped at a red light, the windows of an all-night diner catch my eye. Coffee might be good. Across the street from the diner, the Goldpoint Casino's sign blinks red and gold, beckoning. Casinos have coffee, right?

The light turns green, and I should drive straight home. I should go to bed like the good wife I am and wake up tomorrow to the same empty routine.

I turn left into the casino parking lot.

I park and watch people enter and exit through glass doors. They're wearing jeans and t-shirts and laughing loudly. They all look to be having a better time than I had at the gala.

When I flip down the visor mirror, the woman looking back at me belongs in the Wellington Foundation Gala, not here. Yeah, that needs to change.

I dig through my clutch and pull out my makeup. Using the mirror, I darken my eyeshadow into a smoky haze. I layer mascara until my lashes are thick and dark. The pink lipstick disappears under deep crimson.

My hair completes the transformation. I drag my fingers through it until it falls in messy, wild waves. The woman in the mirror now looks like she's capable of things the charity gala version would never dream of.

What am I even doing? I don't gamble anymore, and I definitely don't visit casinos in questionable neighborhoods. I'm Shannon Matthews, member of the country club and three different charity boards. I don't do spontaneity.

But maybe that's exactly the problem.

The casino parking lot stretches before me like a border between worlds. I grab my phone, intending to slide it into my clutch, but the reality of what I'm about to do hits me. A woman alone at a casino at night—Robert should know. I text him.

SHANNON:

> Hey, I stopped at a casino on the way home. Don't worry, I'm just grabbing coffee. Maybe I'll play a hand of poker if they have a table.

His response is quicker than expected.

ROBERT:

> A casino? Which one?

SHANNON:

> Goldpoint. Not our usual scene.

ROBERT:

> Are you all right? I thought you were going home to bed.

SHANNON:

> Yeah, I just needed to do something outside the routine.

Three dots appear, disappear, then reappear. When his message comes through, my stomach tightens.

ROBERT:

> You should do more spontaneous things. How do you look? Still in your gala dress?

I catch my reflection in the mirror and smile.

SHANNON:

> Same dress, but I did some creative makeup work in the car.

ROBERT:

> Show me.

The command sends an unexpected jolt of desire through me. I like it when he takes control. I angle the phone, ensuring the lighting captures my transformed appearance, and snap a selfie. I look like a sluttier version of myself.

Before I second-guess myself, I hit send.

ROBERT:

> Holy fuck. You look incredible, babe. Like someone I'd want to take home.

SHANNON:

> That's the point.

ROBERT:

> If you see someone you like in there, go for it. You have my permission to have fun. Enjoy yourself.

I read the message twice, recalling our conversation three nights ago. Seeing it in text makes it real.

SHANNON:

> You're serious?

ROBERT:

> Yes. Your pleasure is the sexiest thing in the world to me. All of it. Even the parts with someone else. Just tell me everything afterwards.

His response warms me.

SHANNON:

> You might regret saying that.

ROBERT:

> No way. Go explore. Come home and tell me everything. I'll be waiting.

The messages remind me of our flirting when we first met. I send him a kissy emoji, then pause as I'm about to drop the phone into my purse.

The streetlamp catches my wedding ring—three carats of flawless diamond surrounded by smaller stones. Without analyzing the decision, I twist it off my finger. The band leaves a pale indent on my skin. I stare at the naked finger, then drop both phone and ring into my purse with a decisive snap of the clasp.

I know I'm not going to find someone to fuck at the casino. That's just not me. But this impulsive stop has already spiced things up for us, and I haven't even gotten out of the car.

Now it's time to see what a little gambling does for me.

Chapter 2

I push open the door to the casino, and a security guard nods politely. He doesn't know who I am or who I'm married to. He doesn't care about the Wellington Foundation Gala or which charity boards I sit on. The anonymity is intoxicating.

The carpet is garish and the lighting harsh. The air reeks of cheap perfume and desperation. People hunch over gaming tables scattered across the floor, but the poker room is behind glass walls at the back, an aquarium for serious players. I haven't played since college, but I'm still drawn to it.

The host at the poker room entrance smiles in greeting. "Haven't seen you here before."

"It's my first time. I'd like to play."

"What's your game?"

"Texas Hold'em."

She nods toward a table with five players. "Buy-in is fifty minimum. You want to start there?"

I scan the table. They all look to be working-class regulars and late-night gamblers. Suddenly, my dress feels like a costume. So what if I don't fit in.

"Sure." I pull cash from my purse and hand it to her.

When I sit down and get dealt in, the cards feel familiar in my hands. I have a pair of eights—not bad for a starting hand.

The first few hands pass quickly. I fold most of them and use the time to study the other players. An older man in a work shirt touches his wedding ring when he's nervous. A young woman with piercings taps her fingers when she's bluffing. A guy in his mid-30s watches everyone else more than his cards.

I win a small pot, lose one, then win another. The rhythm returns, like muscle memory. For the first time in months,

I'm not thinking about tomorrow's schedule or the next charity obligation. I'm just present.

That's when everything shifts.

All at once, the poker room goes quiet. Conversations die mid-sentence. Even the dealer's hands freeze above the felt.

I turn in my seat.

The man walking toward our table doesn't announce his authority. He wears it. Dark hair with distinguished silver at the temples frames sharp features. His black polo stretches across broad shoulders, and an expensive watch gleams on his wrist. But it's his eyes that catch me. He's assessing me like I'm prey he's decided is worth the hunt, and arousal hits me like a physical force.

When our eyes lock, I grip the table edge. I should look away. I don't.

"Evening, folks." His voice carries easily across the poker room. Not loud but commanding enough to make everyone listen.

The other players straighten. The dealer nods with clear respect.

He stops beside our table. His dark eyes are fixed on me. "Rough night?"

I gesture at my modest chip stack. "Actually, I'm doing okay."

His mouth curves, but it's not quite a smile. "The night's young, and the cards can turn on you." He extends his hand. "I'm Tony." When I take it, his palm is warm and slightly rough. Working hands, despite the expensive watch and his polished exterior. "I manage this place."

"Shannon." My name feels different, stripped of all the Mrs. Robert Matthews associations.

"Shannon." He repeats it slowly. "It's your first time here. I would've remembered you."

My heart is racing, and I try to hide how he's turning me on. "Should I be flattered or concerned?"

"Depends on how much you like taking risks."

Before I can respond, Tony nods to the dealer. The dealer immediately shifts, creating space at the table. When Tony settles into the chair next to me, the other players become background noise.

"Mind if I watch a few rounds?" I don't reply because we both know my answer doesn't matter. Why do I find that so sexy?

The game resumes, but everything has changed. When I lean forward, my dress clings to my curves. I can feel Tony's gaze on me.

I pick up my next hand and struggle to focus on the cards. The other players make their bets carefully, fold more often, and avoid drawing Tony's attention.

The flop shows ten of spades, jack of clubs, queen of diamonds. I have a king and an ace—a straight draw, and I need a nine or an ace to complete it.

I push chips forward. "Two hundred."

The turn card is a four of hearts. No help, but I'm pot-committed now. Tony's forearms flex when he shifts position, and I notice a thin scar on his left hand.

The river brings a six of diamonds. Nothing. I have ace-high and a prayer. The bet is risky.

The pierced woman studies me for a moment, then folds. I win the pot, but Tony's expression suggests he knows I was bluffing.

"Not bad. But when you're playing with fire, eventually, you'll get burned."

Something low in my stomach tightens. I force myself to look at my cards. We play three more hands. I win one and lose two. Tony's attention never wavers, and my bets grow reckless.

When I go all-in on a pair of jacks and get called by three of a kind, my stack of chips shrinks to almost nothing.

"Luck's turning," Tony's tone is almost sympathetic.

I buy another hundred dollars' worth of chips.

And another.

When my stack dwindles again, I signal the dealer. "Another hundred."

The dealer glances at my remaining chips, then at me. "Cash or card?"

"I'll settle up at the end." The words come out smoothly, like I've said them before.

The dealer hesitates and his eyes flick toward Tony.

Tony gives a single, almost imperceptible nod. The dealer slides a fresh stack of chips across the felt without another word. No questions. No payment required. Just Tony's silent approval, and suddenly the rules don't apply to me.

The power of it sends a thrill down my spine.

Tony leans back in his chair. "You sure you can afford those bets? I've seen your type here before. People who look wealthy but can't cover their losses."

He thinks I'm pretending to be wealthy. I could laugh and tell him I can cover this table's cost ten times over. But he's being a condescending prick, and god help me, I'm turned on.

Instead, I smile coyly over at him. "Just trying my luck."

Tony's smile sharpens. "Let's see how lucky you are."

Lucky. The word echoes in my head, but I'm not thinking about the cards in my hand. I'm thinking about his hands. About getting lucky in a way that has nothing to do with poker.

The next hour blurs by. I miss obvious tells while stealing glances at Tony. I make poor bets, too distracted by possibility. I chase losses with reckless plays, wondering what other risks I might take tonight.

When the older man across from me lays down a full house that destroys my flush, my chips have nearly vanished.

"How much am I down?"

The dealer replies. "Fifteen hundred."

Fifteen hundred dollars. Less than I spent on shoes last month. I could pay this with my credit card right now.

I eye Tony out of the corner of my eye, and pretend to be disappointed. "Fuck. I didn't expect to lose that much."

Tony stands slowly, and the grace of his movement reminds me of a big cat. "That's how it works. The house always wins." He pauses, his eyes traveling down my body and back up. "We should talk about this. Privately. My office."

My heart pounds as I stand. I can feel the other players' awareness as they carefully avoid looking at us.

I should tell Tony right now that I have the money to settle this debt immediately. That fifteen hundred dollars is pocket change.

But I stay quiet and follow him out of the poker room.

Robert told me to explore. To go for it if I saw something interesting.

I have no idea what I'm doing. But as Tony's hand brushes the small of my back, guiding me toward an elevator, I realize I don't want to stop and figure it out.

CHAPTER 3

THE ELEVATOR ASCENDS IN silence. Tony stands close enough that his expensive, masculine cologne fills the small space. His presence makes the air thick and tense.

My fingers twist around my purse strap. I could stop this, but words form in my head and vanish before reaching my lips.

The doors slide open to reveal a hallway unlike the casino floor. Artwork hangs in expensive frames, and plush carpet swallows our footsteps. The recessed lighting creates soft shadows.

Tony's hand is still on my lower back. The heat of his palm seeps through my dress, sending a current up my spine.

We stop at a door with a brass nameplate that says "Antonio Ricci - Private."

He unlocks it and steps aside. "After you."

The office steals my breath. Floor-to-ceiling windows frame the Seattle skyline. A massive dark wood desk dominates the space. Italian leather furniture invites intimate conversation. A bar cart holds bottles I recognize from Robert's collection—the kind that cost thousands.

The details tell a deeper story. A photograph on the credenza shows Tony shaking hands with a man who bears a striking resemblance to the state senator. A statue of Saint Michael, patron saint of protection and battle, stands on his desk. Whatever Tony manages, it's more than just a casino floor.

"Have a seat." Tony moves to the bar cart. "Drink?"

"Water's fine." My voice is steadier than expected.

I sit down and cross my legs while he pours two glasses from a crystal decanter. When he turns to face me, his eyes scan my body, taking in the slit in my dress that shows my thigh.

"So," he says as he settles into the chair across from me instead of behind his desk. "We have a problem."

My pulse quickens. "The fifteen hundred."

He sips his water, watching me over the rim. "That's a significant amount for most people."

Three words would end this: I can pay. I don't say them.

"It is."

Tony studies me. "You walked in here looking wealthy. That dress, those shoes, the way you carry yourself." His gaze travels up my body slowly. "But I've been in this business a long time. I know the difference between people who have money and those who just look like they do."

The assumption lingers between us.

"You think I can't pay."

"Can you?"

A dark and dangerous thrill simmers in my veins. He thinks I'm someone else. Someone whose hair gets messy from life, not because I ran my fingers through it. Someone who takes risks because she has to, not because she's bored.

I hold his gaze, letting the silence stretch. His eyes darken, and I realize he's not just assessing my financial situation. He's trying to figure out what I'm willing to do about it.

"What if I can't?"

Tony's mouth curves into that not-quite-smile. "Then we'd need to discuss alternative arrangements." He sits back, but his eyes never leave mine. "I'm a reasonable man, Shannon. There are always...options."

Heat pools low in my stomach. My black Amex card is heavy in my purse. One swipe would shatter his certainty.

Instead, I lean back in my chair and mirror his posture. "What kind of options?"

Tony sets down his water glass and leans forward, his dark eyes locking onto mine. "I'll let you work it off...persona lly."

"What does that mean?" I need to hear what he wants before I agree.

"It means you come over here and let me see if you're as stunning without that dress as you are in it. It means you show me how much you want this."

My panties grow damp. Fuck, I do want this. And the fact he thinks I'm willing to trade my body makes it hotter. I could do anything I want tonight, and clearly, my body wants me to be a slut who fucks the casino manager.

My thighs quiver as I stand and place my purse on the chair before moving in front of him.

Tony's completely still except for his eyes tracking every movement. I reach behind me, finding the zipper at the small of my back. The slow rasp of it lowering fills the quiet office, and Tony's jaw tightens.

The dress loosens around my body, but I hold it in place. Making him wait.

"Shannon." His tone holds a warning, like he's about ready to take control and rip my dress off me. Knowing he wants me makes me feel powerful.

I slide one spaghetti strap off my shoulder, then the other. The velvet clings to my breasts for a moment before I let it fall, the fabric pooling at my hips. The cool air hits my skin, and my nipples pebble beneath my black lace strapless bra.

Tony's knuckles tighten on the armrests of his chair. My breathing speeds up, and all my nerve endings zing alive.

He could shove me over his desk right now and fuck me hard. I'd just beg for more.

I shimmy my hips, and the dress slides down my legs, leaving me in nothing but my lingerie and heels. I step out of the crimson circle of fabric and kick it aside.

His eyes drag up my body—from my stilettos, over my thighs, lingering on the black lace barely covering my pussy, and up to my breasts before finally meeting my gaze.

"Do you have any idea how fucking gorgeous you are?" Tony's voice roughens.

My pussy throbs with each heartbeat. I'm nearly naked, while he remains fully clothed, yet I've never felt more in control.

"Touch yourself," he commands, not moving from his chair.

I trail my fingers down my stomach, hesitating at the waistband of my panties. This isn't me—Shannon Matthews doesn't fuck strangers in casino offices. But tonight, I'm not that woman, and I can already tell I'm wetter than I have been in months.

"Now," Tony growls.

My hand slips beneath the lace, and my fingers glide easily between my folds. I moan at the contact as a shiver runs up my spine. It's been over fifteen years since I've fucked another guy, and knowing I'm going into this willingly makes me feel like such a slut. It's glorious.

"Show me your pussy," he says.

I hook my thumbs into my panties and slide them down my thighs. When I step out of them, I spread my legs and silently thank the universe that I recently waxed. I'm nice and tidy with a small patch of hair that does nothing to hide my pussy.

Tony rises from his chair with predatory grace. He circles me slowly, his gaze burning across every inch of exposed skin. When he stops behind me, his breath warms my neck.

"Your husband is a lucky man." His fingers trace my spine, barely touching.

My breath catches. "What makes you think I'm married?"

His fingertip taps the pale line on my ring finger. "Experience." His lips brush my ear. "Does he know where you are?"

I'm truthful, but I don't tell him everything. "He knows I'm at the casino. He doesn't know about this."

Tony's hand slides around to cup my breast, thumb grazing my nipple through the lace. "And he lets you play these games?"

"I've never done this before." My voice is breathless, barely recognizable.

"Interesting." Tony unclasps my bra, and it falls to the floor. "Turn around."

I pivot to face him, my nipples hardening further under his intense scrutiny. His hand cups my jaw, thumb pressing against my lower lip.

"Open."

I part my lips, and he slides his thumb into my mouth. I taste salt and skin as I suck gently.

"Good girl." His approval sends a rush of heat between my legs. "Now, get on your knees."

I sink down, the plush carpet cushioning my knees. My hands reach for his belt, but he catches my wrists.

"Not yet. Tell me what you want."

My pussy clenches, and I practically moan, "I want to suck your cock."

I never talk like this with Robert, but it feels right tonight.

Tony releases my wrists and threads his fingers through my hair, gripping firmly. "Then earn it."

I unbuckle his belt, my fingers trembling with anticipation. The button of his slacks pops free, and I lower his zipper with agonizing slowness. His erection strains against black boxer briefs, the outline impressive.

I pull down both layers, freeing his cock. It's thick and hard, jutting proudly from a nest of dark hair. A drop of pre-cum glistens at the tip.

My mouth waters. I lean forward, maintaining eye contact as I lick the bead of moisture from his head. His taste is salty and masculine.

"Fuck," he hisses, his grip tightening in my hair.

I take him into my mouth, my lips stretching around his girth. My tongue swirls around his head before I slide down his shaft, taking as much as I can.

"Jesus Christ," Tony groans, his hips jerking forward slightly.

I establish a rhythm, my hand working what won't fit in my mouth. His cock pulses against my tongue as I hollow my cheeks, sucking harder.

Tony's breathing grows ragged. "Stop," he commands suddenly, pulling me off him. "Stand up."

I rise on shaky legs. His eyes darken as he steps closer, crowding me against the desk. The heat radiating from his body makes my skin prickle with anticipation.

He cups my face with one hand, his thumb tracing my lower lip, still wet from sucking his cock. "You're something else, Shannon."

Before I can respond, his mouth crashes against mine. The kiss is nothing like Robert's—it's demanding, almost punishing. His tongue pushes past my lips, claiming me. I've never been kissed like this, and the realization sends a jolt straight to my core.

His lips break from mine and trail down my neck. His stubble scrapes against my sensitive skin as his teeth graze my pulse point. When he latches onto my neck, I gasp. He sucks hard, marking me, and my knees nearly buckle.

"Fuck," I whisper, my fingers digging into his shoulders. The slight pain mixed with pleasure has my pussy throbbing. The thought of walking around with Tony's brand on my skin makes me dizzy with arousal.

He pulls back to inspect his work, satisfaction evident in his expression. "Now everyone will see how much of a slut you are."

The hickey throbs. Robert will see it. The thought should terrify me, but instead, it sends another rush of wetness between my legs.

Tony spins me around and bends me over his desk in one fluid motion. My breasts press against the cool wood, papers scattering beneath me.

His hand lands on my ass with a sharp crack. The sting blooms across my skin, and I cry out—not in pain but surprise mingled with pleasure.

"You like that?" His voice is knowing.

My body answers before my mouth can—a shudder racing through me. Who is this woman taking over my body? Certainly not Shannon Matthews, charity board member. This is someone who craves the sting of a man's palm against her ass.

"Yes," I gasp, arching into his touch.

He spanks me again, harder this time. The sharp crack echoes in the room, and my pussy clenches around nothing, desperate to be filled. Holy fuck. I've never been spanked before. Never wanted it. Yet here I am, practically dripping with need.

"Please," I whimper.

My voice sounds desperate. I'm becoming someone new under his hands, someone who begs. The proper wife is dissolving with each stinging slap, replaced by a woman who wants to be used.

"Please what?" His fingers graze the stinging spot on my ass.

The gentle touch after the pain makes me dizzy with desire. I should be embarrassed by how quickly I'm surrendering to him, how eagerly I'm sinking into submission. Instead, I'm leaning into it, craving more. Would Robert recognize me right now? His sophisticated wife is being transformed into this wanton creature.

"Fuck me. Please fuck me."

The words fall from my lips without hesitation. I've become the sluttiest version of myself, and I don't care. I want his cock inside me more than I want my next breath. My body hums with a need I've never felt before.

Tony chuckles, the sound dark and promising. "Not yet."

He slides his hand between my legs from behind, fingers parting my folds. "So wet," he murmurs appreciatively. "Is this all for me?"

"Yes," I moan as his middle finger circles my entrance.

He pushes two fingers inside me without warning, and my body welcomes the intrusion. My inner walls clench around him as he curls his fingers, finding that perfect spot.

"Oh god," I gasp, my hips bucking against his hand.

"You're going to come for me first," he says as he brings his other hand up to rub my clit. "Then I'll fuck you."

His fingers work me expertly, pumping in and out while he brushes circles around my swollen bud. The dual sensation builds rapidly, my orgasm approaching with startling speed.

"I'm close," I pant, clutching the edge of the desk.

"Look at me," Tony demands.

I glance over my shoulder, meeting his intense gaze.

"I want to see your face when you come."

His words push me over the edge. My orgasm crashes through me, my pussy spasms rhythmically around his fingers as waves of pleasure radiate outward. I cry out, breaking eye contact as my head drops to the desk. I just orgasmed for someone other than my husband. And I want more.

"Beautiful," Tony murmurs, working me through the aftershocks.

Before I can recover, I feel the head of his cock pressing against my pussy.

"Tell me you want this," he demands.

"I want you," I gasp. "Fuck me."

He pushes forward, stretching me deliciously as he enters in one slow thrust. Fuuuck. In my mouth, he didn't seem that much bigger than Robert, but right now, it feels like he's splitting me open. I feel impossibly full, my body adjusting to his size.

"God, you're tight," he groans. "I could fuck this pussy all night long."

He grasps my hips, pulling almost all the way out before driving back in.

"Ooooh, god!" I squeal in pleasure. Each thrust sends shockwaves of delight through my body, my sensitive pussy still tingling from my orgasm. "Harder," I beg, pushing back against him.

Tony laughs darkly and increases his pace. The sound of skin slapping against skin fills the office, punctuated by our heavy breathing and my continual moans.

My second orgasm builds, coiling tight in my lower belly. Tony's fingers dig into my hips, hard enough to leave marks—marks I'll have to explain to Robert. The thought of telling my husband about this sends a fresh surge of arousal through me.

"You close again?" Tony's voice is strained, his rhythm faltering slightly.

"Yes," I gasp. "Don't stop."

"I'm not stopping until I'm done using you."

His words make me whimper in pleasure. I never knew I'd enjoy being talked to this way, but it's so fucking hot.

He reaches around, his fingers finding my clit. The added stimulation is too much. My orgasm explodes through me, more intense than the first. My pussy clamps down on his cock, and I cry out as sparkles of light burst behind my eyelids.

I'm floating in a happy, fuzzy place, and I expect Tony to come any moment, but instead, he pulls out and flips me over. The cool wood of the desk is a shock against my heated back as he lifts my legs onto his shoulders. My black heels on my feet almost look obscene on the shoulders of anyone other than my husband.

"I want to see your face when I fill you with my cum," he says, his voice raw with desire.

He slides back inside me, and this new angle allows him to go deeper than before. Each thrust hits a spot inside me that sends pleasure radiating through my entire body.

His dark eyes lock onto mine. "Your husband ever fuck you like this?"

"No," I moan, and it's the truth. Robert is considerate and skilled, but he's never fucked me on a desk. He's never made me feel like I'm just there for his pleasure. This is new territory.

"Good." Tony's pace quickens, his movements becoming more erratic. "This pussy is mine tonight."

"Yours," I agree, lost in the pleasure.

With a final, deep thrust, Tony groans, and I feel him pulse inside me, his cum painting my insides. The sensation triggers another smaller orgasm, and I writhe as pleasure ripples from my fingertips to my toes.

We stay connected for a moment, the only sound our ragged breathing. When he finally pulls out, I feel his cum leak out of me, dripping onto the desk below. I can't believe I just let a stranger come inside me.

Tony tucks himself away and zips up his pants, looking remarkably composed for someone who just fucked me senseless. He extends a hand to help me up. My legs shake so badly I stumble into his chest.

"Easy there," he says, steadying me with hands on my waist.

He retrieves my dress and bra from the floor and hands it to me. "Get dressed."

I move to grab my panties, but he stops me. "Your panties stay here."

Fuck, that's hot.

I put my bra on and slip the dress over my head. My body hums with satisfaction, and my mind is a whirlwind of emotions. I can't believe I just fucked someone.

"Are you going to be okay driving home?"

I blink at him to clear the fog of lust. "Yes."

He walks me to the door. "Thank you for an enjoyable time."

I've never fucked someone and just left. This feels oddly wrong, yet I know Robert is waiting for me.

He opens the door and kisses me softly. When we break apart, I whisper, "Goodbye."

As I walk to the elevator, my dress clinging to my still-sensitive skin, I feel his eyes following me.

I stop in the restroom downstairs. As I clean up, I catch my reflection in the mirror. My mascara is smudged, my lips swollen, my hair a tangled mess. A purple mark blooms on my collarbone, the size of a man's mouth. I trace it with my fingertip, and my breath catches as the tender skin responds.

I look like a woman who just got thoroughly fucked in a casino office. And I've never felt more alive.

My phone vibrates in my purse as soon as I slide into the car. It's Robert.

ROBERT:

Having fun?

My lips curve into a smile as I type my response.

SHANNON:

You have no idea. I have so much to tell you. I'm in the car and will be there soon.

I drop the phone on the passenger seat. It's time to go home and find out how much my husband wanted this.

CHAPTER 4

THE HOUSE IS SILENT when I come inside from the garage. The familiar lemon and fresh flower scent should calm me, but all I can smell is sex on my skin. My thighs are sticky with a stranger's cum, and I'm walking into the house not totally sure how my husband is going to react. Please, please, please be okay with this.

"Shannon?" Robert's voice calls from upstairs, tight with urgency.

"I'm home." My voice sounds husky, unfamiliar.

I kick my heels off in the entryway and climb the stairs slowly, pausing in the bedroom doorway.

Robert sits on our bed, still in his tuxedo pants and unbuttoned shirt. His bow tie hangs loose around his neck. His eyes widen as they travel over me—lingering on the hickey, wrinkled dress, and smudged mascara.

"Holy shit." His voice drops to a whisper. "Look at you."

I stay in the doorway. "What do you see?"

Robert stands slowly. "I see..." His gaze travels from my tangled hair to my bare feet. "I see my wife. Really see her. For the first time in years."

I step forward. The air crackles with tension. "And?"

"And she's fucking magnificent."

My chest tightens. I move closer until I can feel the heat radiating from his body and smell the whiskey on his breath.

"Tell me." His voice is rough. His fingers reach for the strap of my dress but stop just short of touching me. "Tell me everything that happened."

I smile slowly. "Everything? That will take some time."

His hands finally slide up my bare arms, giving me goosebumps. "We have all night, and I want every detail."

His mouth claims mine, and I taste whiskey and desperation. His hands tangle in my hair—hair that another man gripped an hour ago. Robert's touch feels both familiar and new, as if we're meeting for the first time.

When we break apart, we're both breathless. Robert's eyes are dark with something I haven't seen in years—unadulterated desire. Not the comfortable affection we've fallen into but raw hunger.

"The casino," he prompts, his thumb tracing my jawline. "Start there."

My stomach flutters. "I caught the manager's eye. His name is Tony. He took me to his office." My voice drops. "He thought I couldn't cover my gambling debt."

Robert's breath catches. "You didn't tell him you could?"

"He had no idea who I was." A thrill runs through me. "He offered me an alternative arrangement."

"Fucking hell," Robert mutters, his hands tightening on my hips.

"He told me to strip," I continue, my voice growing more confident. "So I did. Right there in front of his desk."

Robert groans and pulls me flush against him. His erection presses against my stomach. "Then what?"

"He spanked me. Hard."

Robert stills. His eyes search mine. "Did you like it?"

I nod slowly, expecting judgment. Instead, his pupils dilate with excitement. "Show me how you were positioned."

I turn and lift my hair, exposing the back of my neck. Robert slides the zipper down slowly. The fabric pools at my feet. He groans when he sees I'm not wearing panties.

I leave my bra on and move to the bed, bending over the side. I glance over my shoulder to watch him.

"Christ," Robert whispers as he traces the curve of my ass. "You really liked it?"

"Yes." I wiggle my ass at him, and he spanks me experimentally, making me gasp in pleasure. Yeah, my husband would never be able to spank me as hard as Tony did, but that's one of the reasons I love Robert. There's not a mean bone in his body.

"Then what?" Robert's voice is husky, and I can tell this is affecting him as much as it is me.

"Then he made me come."

Robert's hand slides between my legs, fingers exploring my sensitive folds.

"I made him come too," I whisper, meeting his intense gaze. "He came inside me."

"This is from him?"

"Yes," I admit, spreading my legs wider as a bolt of lust zips through me. "I didn't clean up completely."

"Fuck," he groans as he slides his fingers inside me easily. "Don't stop." His breathing grows ragged, and his hands explore more freely. "What else?"

"He fucked me, bent over, until I came." The details flow more easily now.

Robert finger fucks me and murmurs, "He was lucky to have one night."

His words unlock something in me. "He laid me across his desk, and fucked me with my ankles on his shoulder."

Robert groans and pulls his hand from my pussy. He starts stripping. "How did it feel?"

The truth spills out. "Different. Rougher. More...like he was using my body." I watch his face transform with each word. "He gripped my hips hard enough to bruise. Made the desk shake. Made me moan like a slut."

"And then you came home to me." His voice carries an edge I've never heard before.

I wiggle my ass again, desperate for him to fuck me. "I'll always come home to you."

"Fuck." Robert's control slips. "I need you. Now. Need to be inside you, need to—"

He pulls me up, and we tumble onto the bed, limbs tangling, mouths seeking. He kisses me roughly, and I match his intensity. This is fifteen years of history ignited by something new.

He positions himself between my legs, and when he pushes inside, we cry out together.

He gasps. "Shannon, you feel…"

As he fucks me, words fail him. The rhythm turns urgent. It's not lovemaking, it's more primal.

"More," he demands between strokes. "Tell me what it felt like with him inside you."

The request sends electricity through my veins. "Different. He hit different—oh god, right there."

Robert shifts his angle, hitting the spot that blurs my vision. "Like that?"

"Yes." I writhe under him. "Exactly that. He couldn't—only you know how to—"

"Damn right." His thrusts quicken. "You're mine. Fuck whoever you want, but you're always mine."

The possessiveness mixed with permission intoxicates me. "Always yours." My nails dig crescents into his shoulders. "I'll always come back to you."

"Did you think about this?" His voice strains. "When he was inside you, did you imagine telling me later?"

"Yes." No point hiding now. "I couldn't wait for this."

"And is it—?" His rhythm falters. "Is this what you wanted?"

"Better." Pressure builds low in my belly. "So much better. I'm about to—"

"Come for me." His command cuts through everything else.

The words shatter me. My orgasm skyrockets me to a higher plane as pure ecstasy turns me into a moaning mess. I cry out his name, and Robert follows instantly, his groan muffled against my neck as he pulses inside me, adding his cum to Tony's.

We collapse together, breath ragged and skin damp. The room spins from pleasure, and I giggle. I've been fucked silly.

"Holy shit," Robert murmurs while his face is pressed against my neck.

"I know." My fingers trace patterns on his back.

We lie tangled together, the magnitude of what just happened settling around us. The ceiling fan turns slow circles above us, cooling our heated skin.

Robert props himself up on one elbow and studies my face. "Shannon."

My pulse quickens at his tone. "What?"

His finger traces the mark on my neck. "If you wanted to go back there..." He pauses, swallows. "If you wanted to see him again..."

I search his expression for signs of reluctance or pain. Instead, I find only curiosity and desire.

"You would be okay with that?"

He brushes hair from my face. "More than okay." He gestures between us. "What we just shared—I've never felt closer to you."

The realization strikes me hard. "Me either."

"So, if you lost at poker again..." His attempt at casualness fails to mask the tension beneath.

"I'll think about it." I match his tone while feeling the weight of his offer.

He pulls me against his chest. We drift towards sleep wrapped in each other's arms. As Robert's breathing deepens, my mind wanders back to the casino. To Tony's dangerous smile and commanding presence.

What would it be like to stroll through those doors knowing exactly what I'm choosing?

I'm not the same woman who walked into that casino tonight. That Shannon Matthews disappeared somewhere between the poker table and Tony's desk. This new version of me, the one with another man's marks on her skin? She's just getting started.

And she's definitely going back.

The End

About Lacey Cross

Lacey Cross is a wife sharing erotica writer with over 100 short stories published since she started in 2021. Her stories emphasize the pleasure found from the wife living her best slut life and embracing the hotwife lifestyle. She explores themes of free use, submissive wives with dominant bulls, BDSM...and oh-so-many men.

www.ingramcontent.com/pod-product-compliance
Lightning Source LLC
Chambersburg PA
CBHW031416310726
48971CB00003B/891